a gift from the animals to thank him for his kindness. And the up with the crown and the thank you letter for the book's e

It wasn't just the ending that caused me a few headaches. When I wrote my first draft of the story, I did so in rhyme. It didn't feel quite right, however, so I tried some different approaches. At one point I wanted an add-on song, but eventually I wrote the story in prose with rhyming sections throughout, almost like a chorus. My editor cut it back and we had the final version. And now George has been the kindest, if perhaps not the smartest, giant in town for twenty years. Maybe he needs some new clothes to celebrate?

Julia Donaldson

Did You Know?

The Smartest Giant in Town has been adapted into a play which was performed at the Little Angel Theatre in London. Here are some photos of the puppets and sets from the play. Who do you recognise from the story?

Why not put on your own play of the story with your friends? You could make your own puppets or even dress up as the characters and act out the story. Don't forget to make a special new crown for George too!

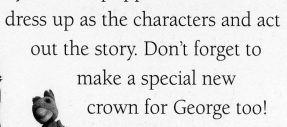

WRITTEN BY
JULIA DONALDSON

ILLUSTRATED BY
AXEL SCHEFFLER

The Smartest GIANT in Town

MACMILLAN CHILDREN'S BOOKS

George was a giant, the scruffiest giant in town.
He always wore the same pair of old brown sandals
and the same old patched-up gown.

"I wish I wasn't the scruffiest giant in town,"
he said sadly.

But one day, George noticed a new shop.

It was full of smart clothes. So he bought . . .

a smart shirt,

a smart pair of trousers,

a smart belt,

a smart stripy tie,

some smart socks
with diamonds up the sides,

and a pair of
smart shiny shoes.

"Now I'm the smartest giant in town," he said proudly.

George left his old clothes
behind in the shop.
He was about to go home
when he heard a sound.

On the pavement stood a giraffe who was sniffing sadly.
"What's the matter?" asked George.

"It's my neck," said the giraffe. "It's so very long and so very cold. I wish I had a long, warm scarf!"

"Cheer up!" said George, and he took off his stripy tie. "It didn't match my socks anyway," he said, as he wound it round and round the giraffe's neck. It made a wonderful scarf.

"Thank you!" said the giraffe.

As George strode towards home, he sang to himself,

"My tie is a scarf for a cold giraffe,

But look me up and down –

I'm the smartest giant in town."

George came to a river. On a boat stood a goat who was
bleating loudly. "What's the matter?" asked George.

"It's my sail," said the goat.

"It blew away in a storm.

"I wish I had a strong new sail for my boat!"

"Cheer up!" said George, and he took off his new white shirt. "It kept coming untucked anyway," he said, as he tied it to the mast of the goat's boat. It made a magnificent sail.

"Thank you!" said the goat.

George strode on, singing to himself,

"My tie is a scarf for a cold giraffe,

My shirt's on a boat as a sail for a goat,

But look me up and down –

I'm the smartest giant in town!"

George came to a tiny ruined house.
Beside the house stood a white mouse with
lots of baby mice. They were all squeaking.
"What's the matter?" asked George.

"It's our house,"
squeaked the mother mouse.

"It burned down, and now
we have nowhere to live.

"I wish we had
a nice new house!"

"Cheer up!" said George, and he took off one of his shiny shoes. "It was giving me blisters anyway," he said, as the mouse and her babies scrambled inside. The shoe made a perfect home for them.

"Thank you!" they squeaked.

George had to hop along the road now, but he didn't mind. As he hopped, he sang to himself,

"My tie is a scarf for a cold giraffe,

My shirt's on a boat as a sail for a goat,

My shoe is a house for a little white mouse,

But look me up and down –

I'm the smartest giant in town."

George came to a campsite.
Beside a tent stood a fox
who was crying.
"What's the matter?"
asked George.

"It's my sleeping bag,"
said the fox.

"I dropped it in a puddle.

"I wish I had a warm, dry sleeping bag!"

"Cheer up!" said George, and he took off one of his socks with diamonds up the sides. "It was tickling my toes anyway," he said, as the fox snuggled into it. It made a very fine sleeping bag.

"Thank you!" said the fox.

George hopped on, singing to himself,

"My tie is a scarf for a cold giraffe,

  My shirt's on a boat as a sail for a goat,

  My shoe is a house for a little white mouse,

One of my socks is a bed for a fox,

  But look me up and down –

  I'm the smartest giant in town."

George came to a big squelchy bog.
Beside the bog stood a dog
who was howling.

"What's the matter?" asked George.

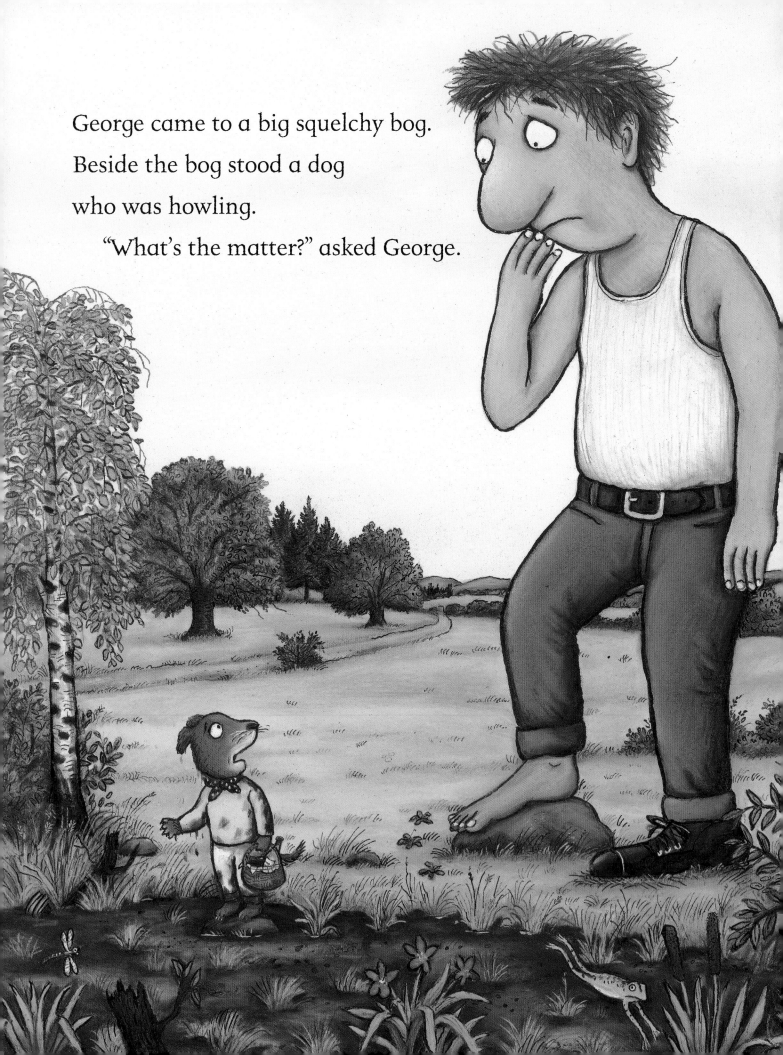

"It's this bog,"
said the dog.

"I need to get across, but I keep
getting stuck in the mud.

"I wish there was
a safe, dry path."

"Cheer up!" said George, and he took off his smart new belt. "It was squashing my tummy anyway," he said, as he laid it down over the bog. It made an excellent path.

"Thank you!" said the dog.

The wind started to blow, but George didn't mind.

He hopped on, singing to himself,

"My tie is a scarf for a cold giraffe,

My shirt's on a boat as a sail for a goat,

My shoe is a house for a little white mouse,

One of my socks is a bed for a fox,

My belt helped a dog who was crossing a bog,

But . . .

"My trousers are falling down!
I'm the coldest giant in town!"

Suddenly George felt sad and shivery and not at all smart.
He stood on one foot and thought. "I'll have to go back
to the shop and buy some more clothes," he decided.
He turned round and hopped all the way back to the shop.

But when he got there, it was CLOSED!

"Oh, no!" cried George. He sank down onto the doorstep
and a tear ran down his nose. He felt as sad as all the animals
he had met on his way home.

Then, out of the corner of his eye, he saw a bag with something
familiar poking out of the top. George took a closer look . . .

"My gown!" he yelled. "My dear old gown and sandals!" George put them on. They felt wonderfully comfortable.

"I'm the cosiest giant in town!" he cried, and he danced back home along the road.

Outside his front door stood all the animals he had helped.
They were carrying an enormous present.

"Come on, George," they said. "Open it!"

George untied the ribbon. Inside was a beautiful gold paper
crown and a card.

"Look inside the card, George!" said the animals.

George put the crown on his head and opened the card.

Inside, it said,

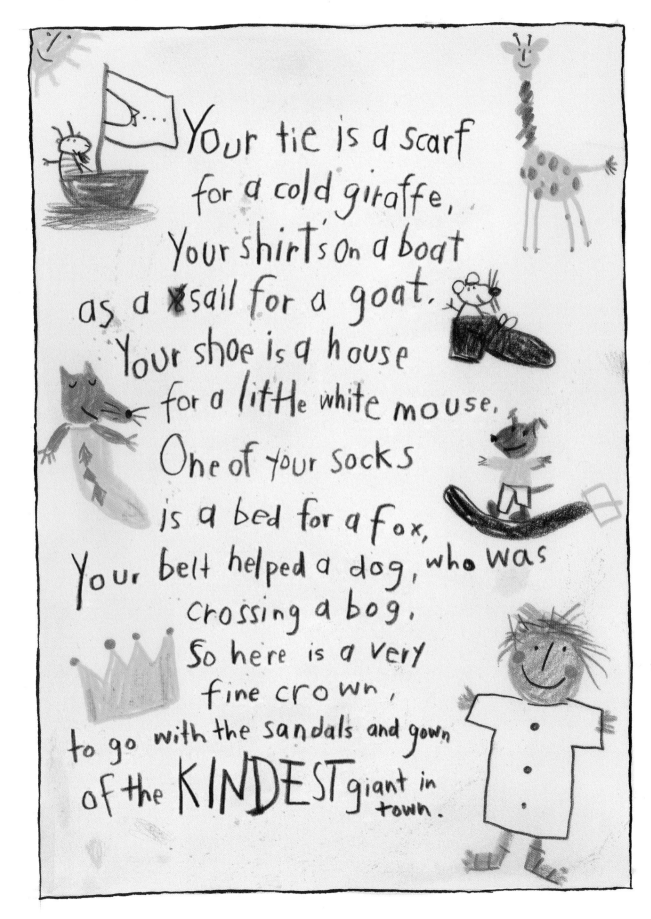

Your tie is a scarf
for a cold giraffe,
Your shirt's on a boat
as a sail for a goat,
Your shoe is a house
for a little white mouse,
One of your socks
is a bed for a fox,
Your belt helped a dog, who was
crossing a bog,
So here is a very
fine crown,
to go with the sandals and gown
of the KINDEST giant in
town.

For Lola – J.D.

First published 2002 by Macmillan Children's Books
This edition published 2022 by Macmillan Children's Books
an imprint of Pan Macmillan
The Smithson, 6 Briset Street, London EC1M 5NR
EU representative: Macmillan Publishers Ireland Ltd
1st Floor, The Liffey Trust Centre,
117–126 Sheriff Street Upper, Dublin 1, D01 YC43
Associated companies throughout the world
www.panmacmillan.com

ISBN: 978-1-5290-7249-5

Text copyright © Julia Donaldson 2002, 2016, 2022
Illustrations copyright © Axel Scheffler 2002, 2022

The Smartest Giant in Town Play photography (page 1) copyright © Ellie Kurttz, courtesy of Little Angel Theatre

1 3 5 7 9 8 6 4 2

A CIP catalogue for this book is available from the British Library.

Printed in China.

Before illustrator Axel Scheffler begins the artwork for a story, he draws some pencil sketches to work out how each page of the book might look. The final illustrations can sometimes look quite different to these early versions.

In Axel's first sketch for the start of *The Smartest Giant in Town*, George the giant was originally wearing trousers and a coat. Then, in this later sketch, Axel gave George his comfy old gown and sandals. He also added lots of extra background characters including two more giants, a lady pushing a pram and even a cat fishing in the fountain! Have a look at the start of the story in this book and see if you can see any of these characters in the finished artwork. Can you spot any differences?

When Axel gets sent one of Julia Donaldson's stories, he also draws sketches of the characters to decide what they might look like. Have a look at these two drawings of the giraffe. Can you see any differences between them? Do either of them look similar to the giraffe in the finished book?